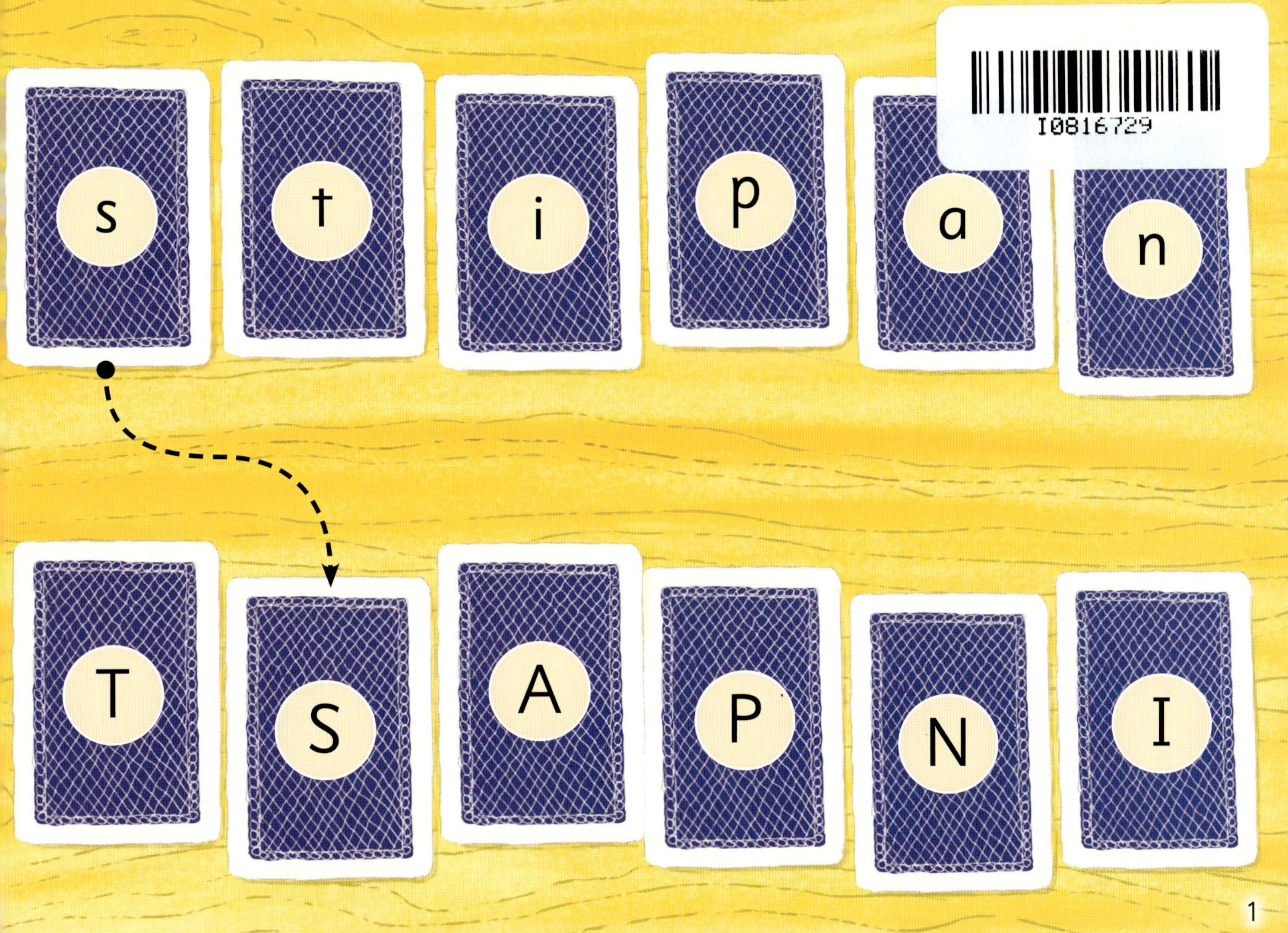
s
t
i
p
a
n
T
S
A
P
N
I

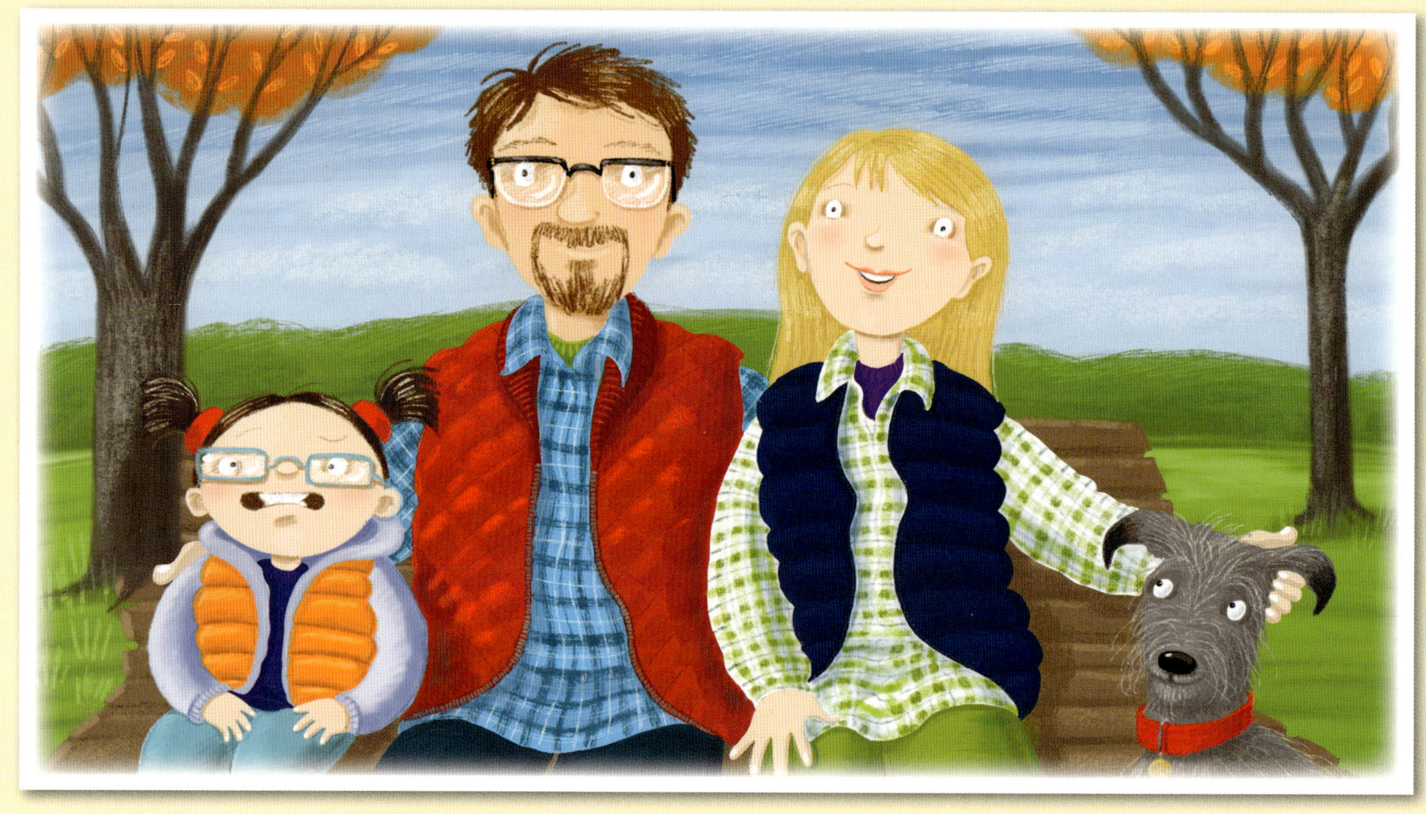

Pip Stan Pat Tips

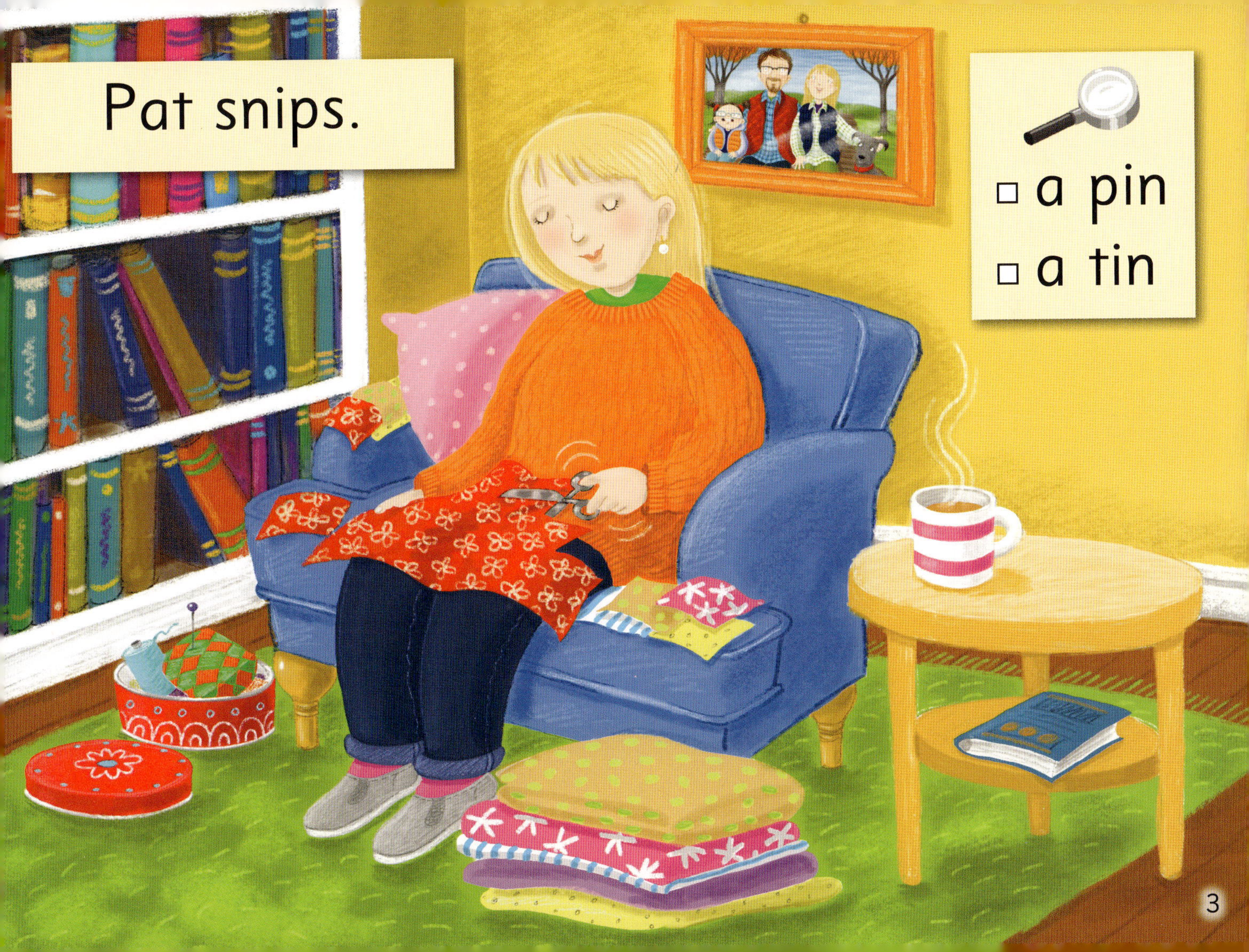
Pat snips.
□ a pin
□ a tin

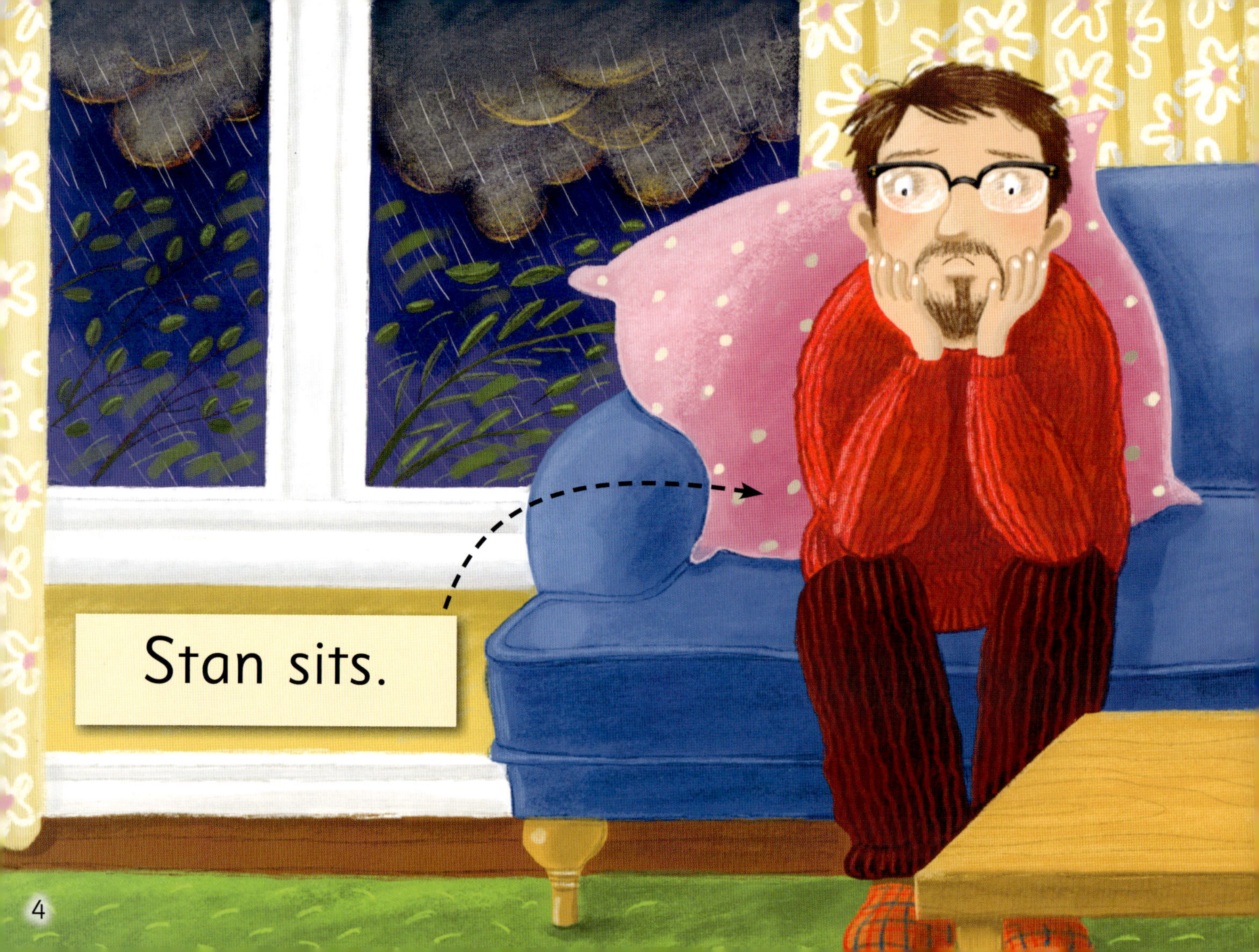
Stan sits.

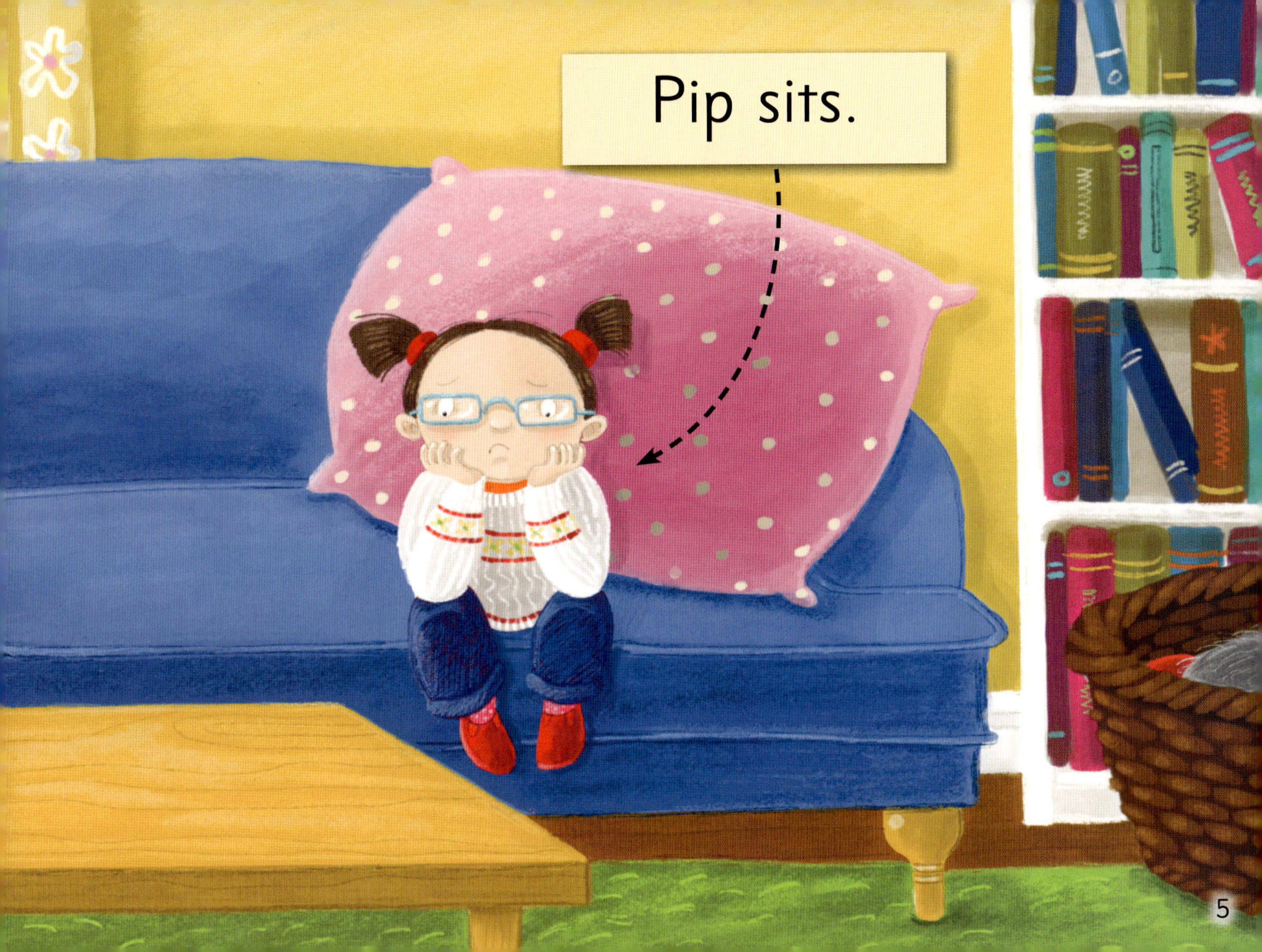
Pip sits.

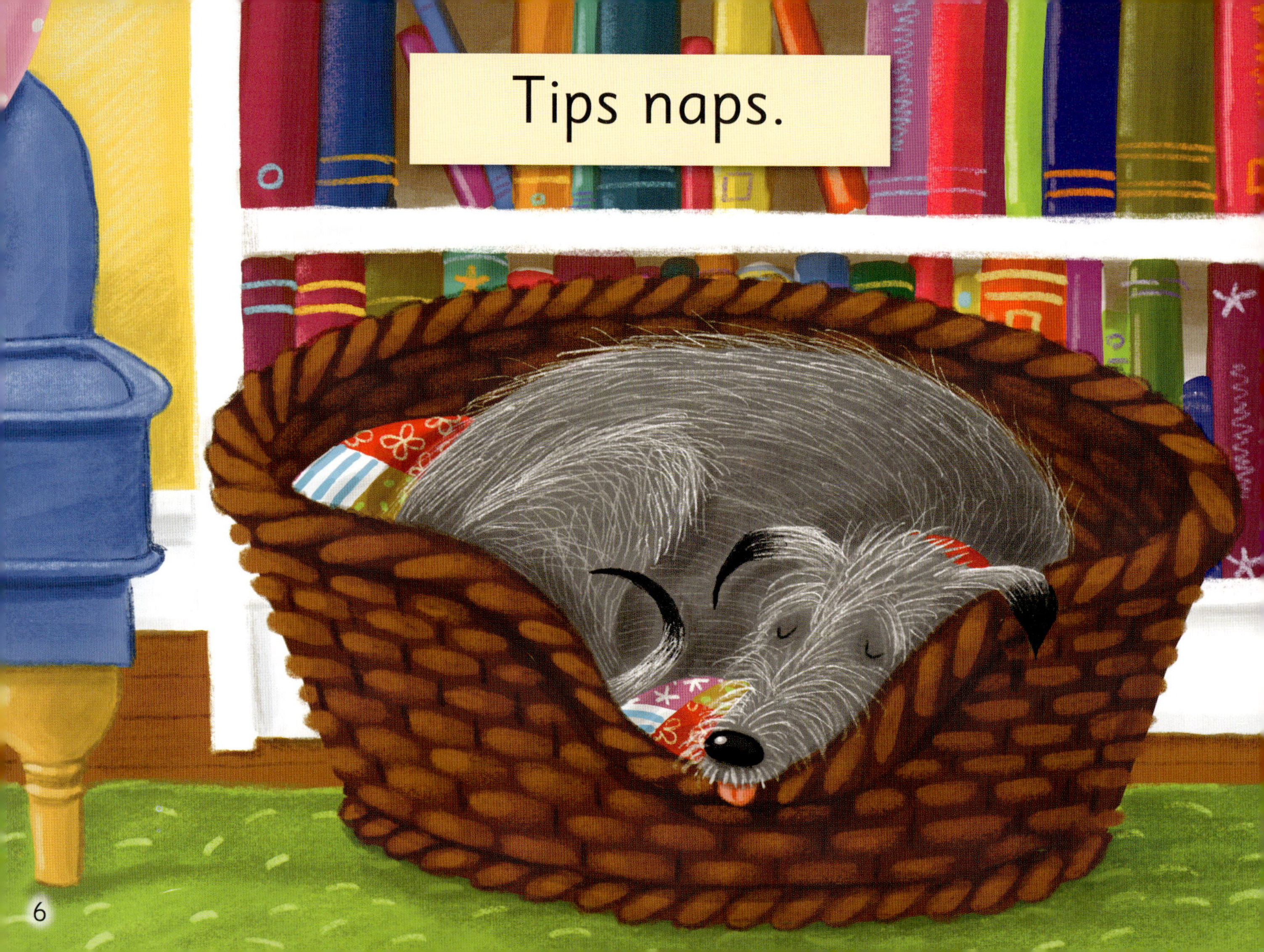

Tips naps.

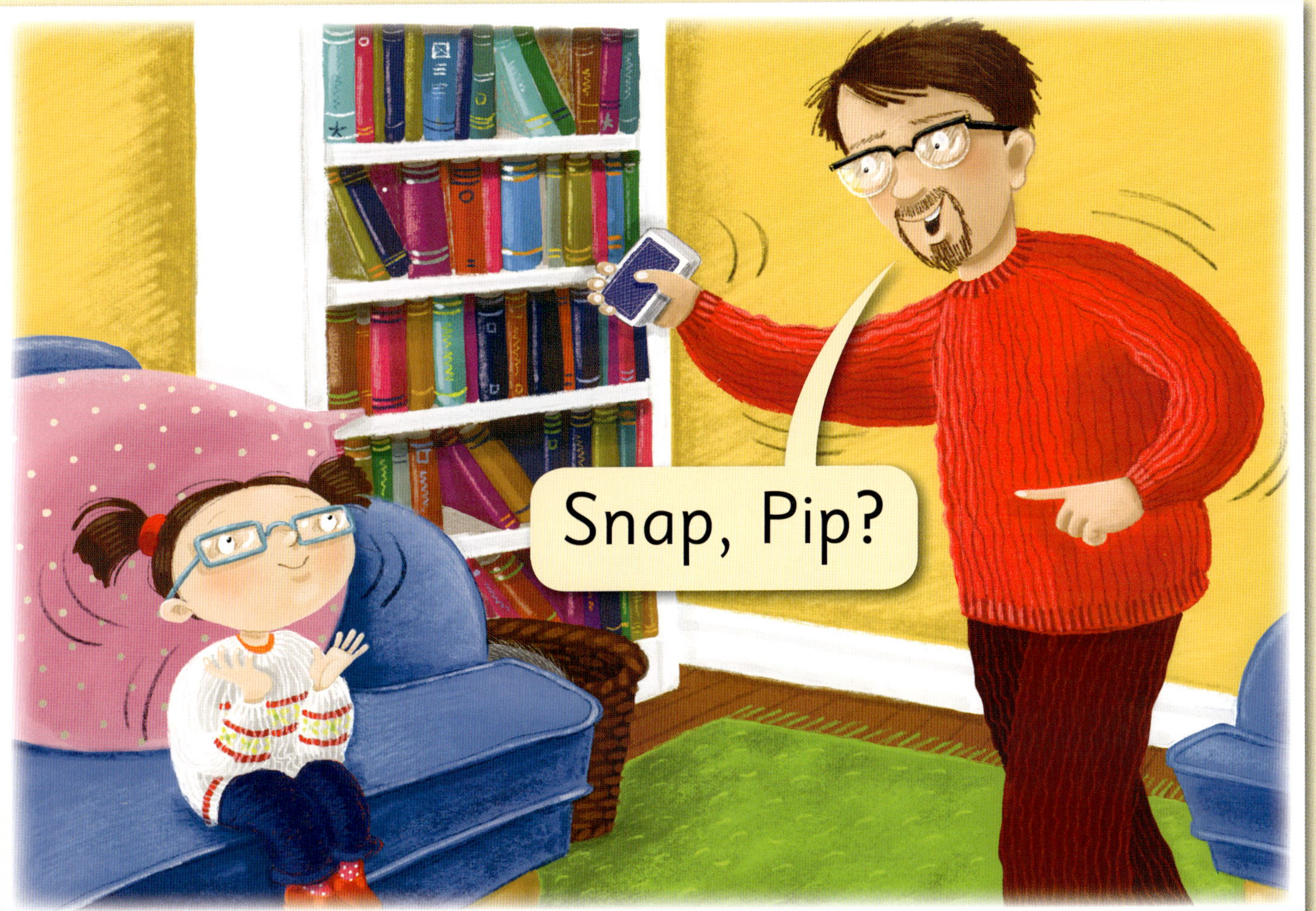
Snap, Pip?

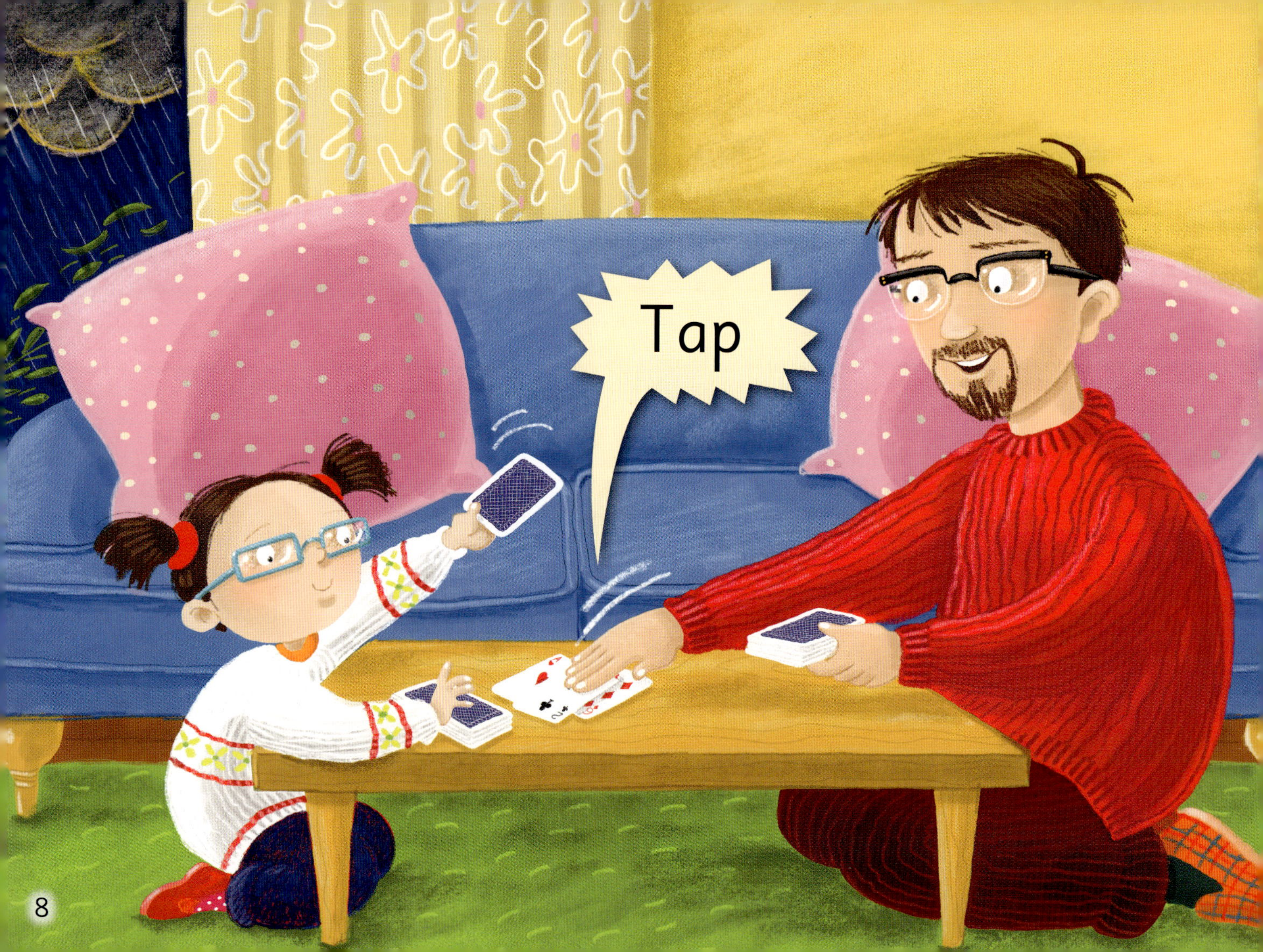
Tap

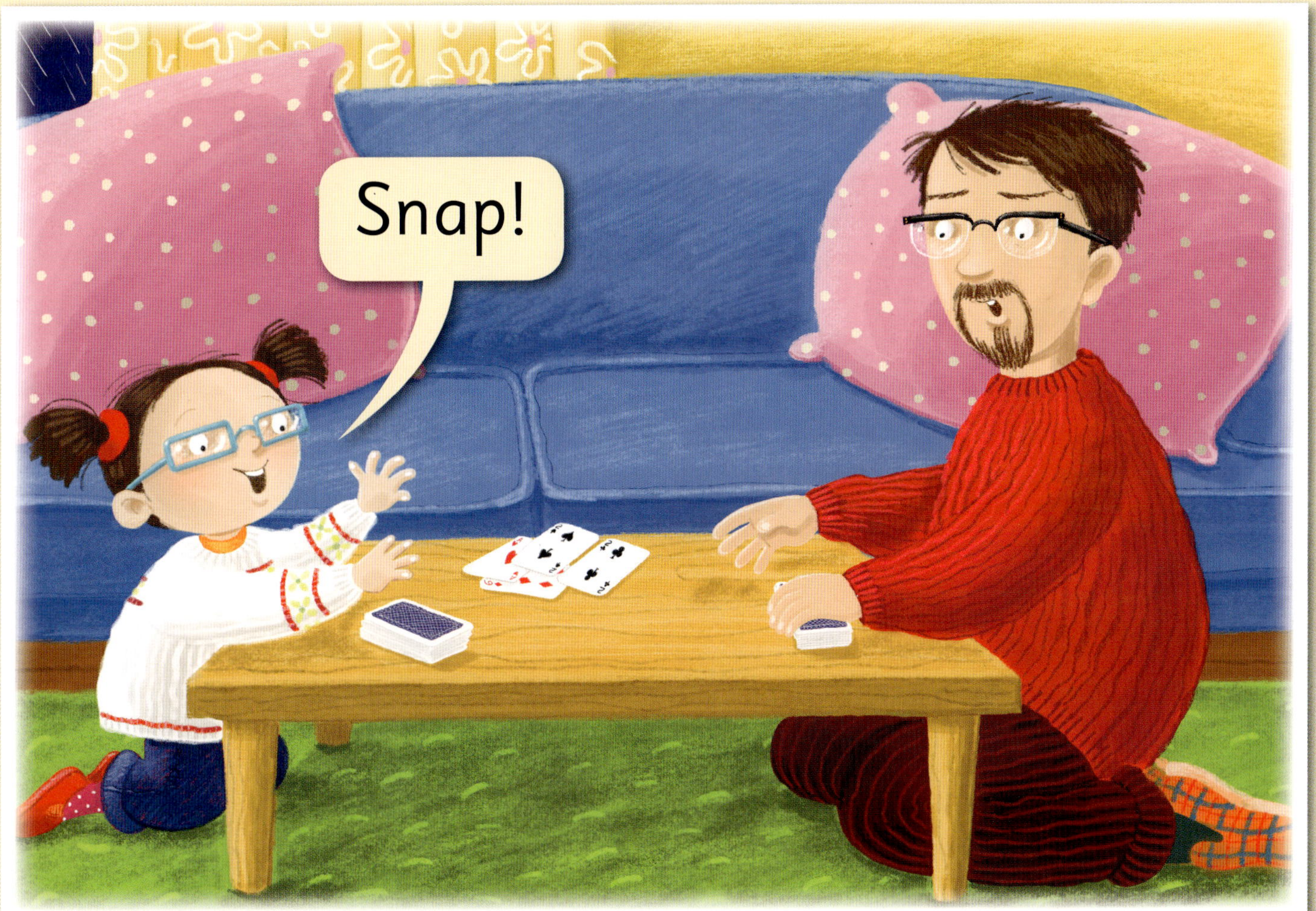
Snap!

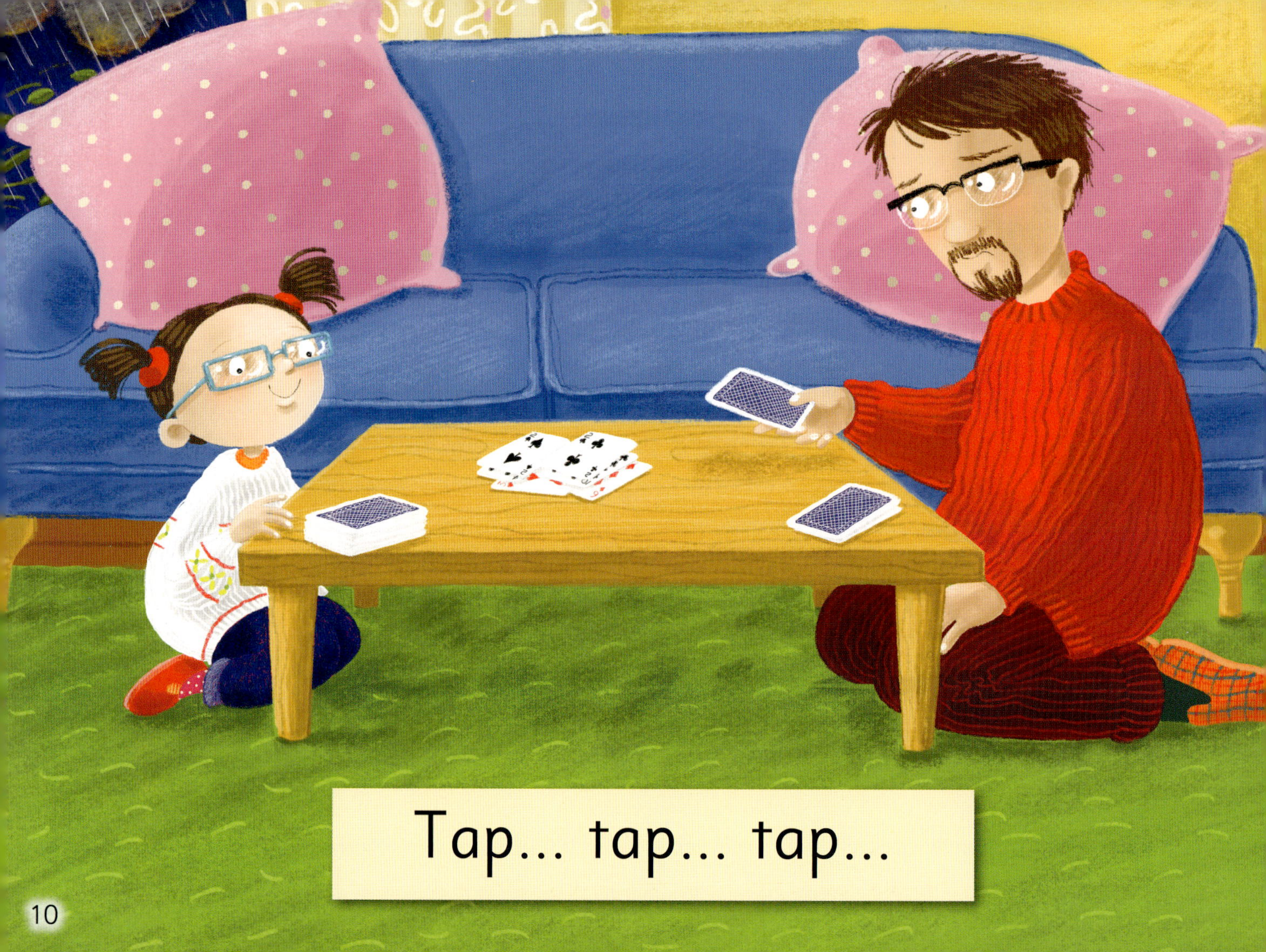

Tap... tap... tap...

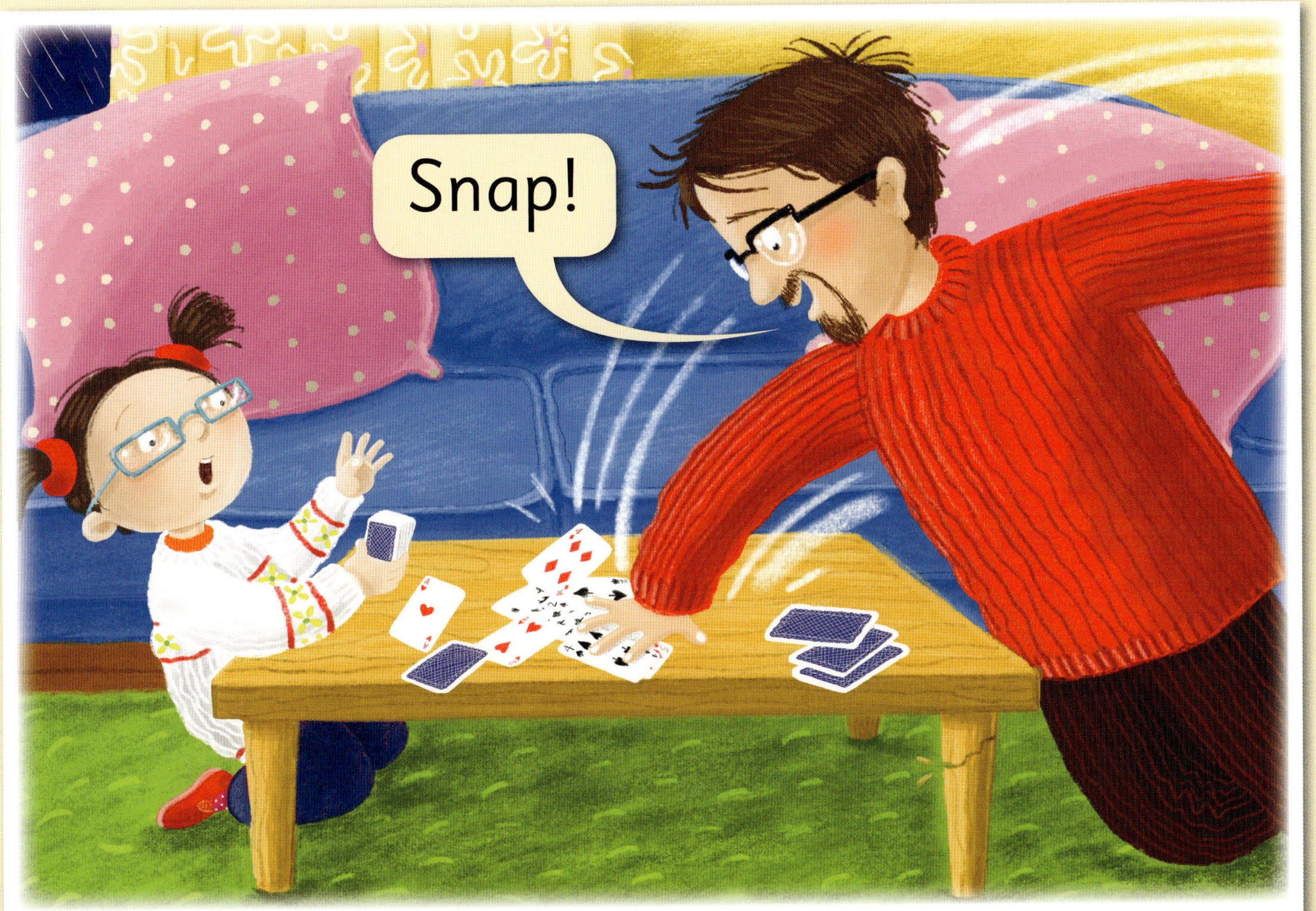
Snap!

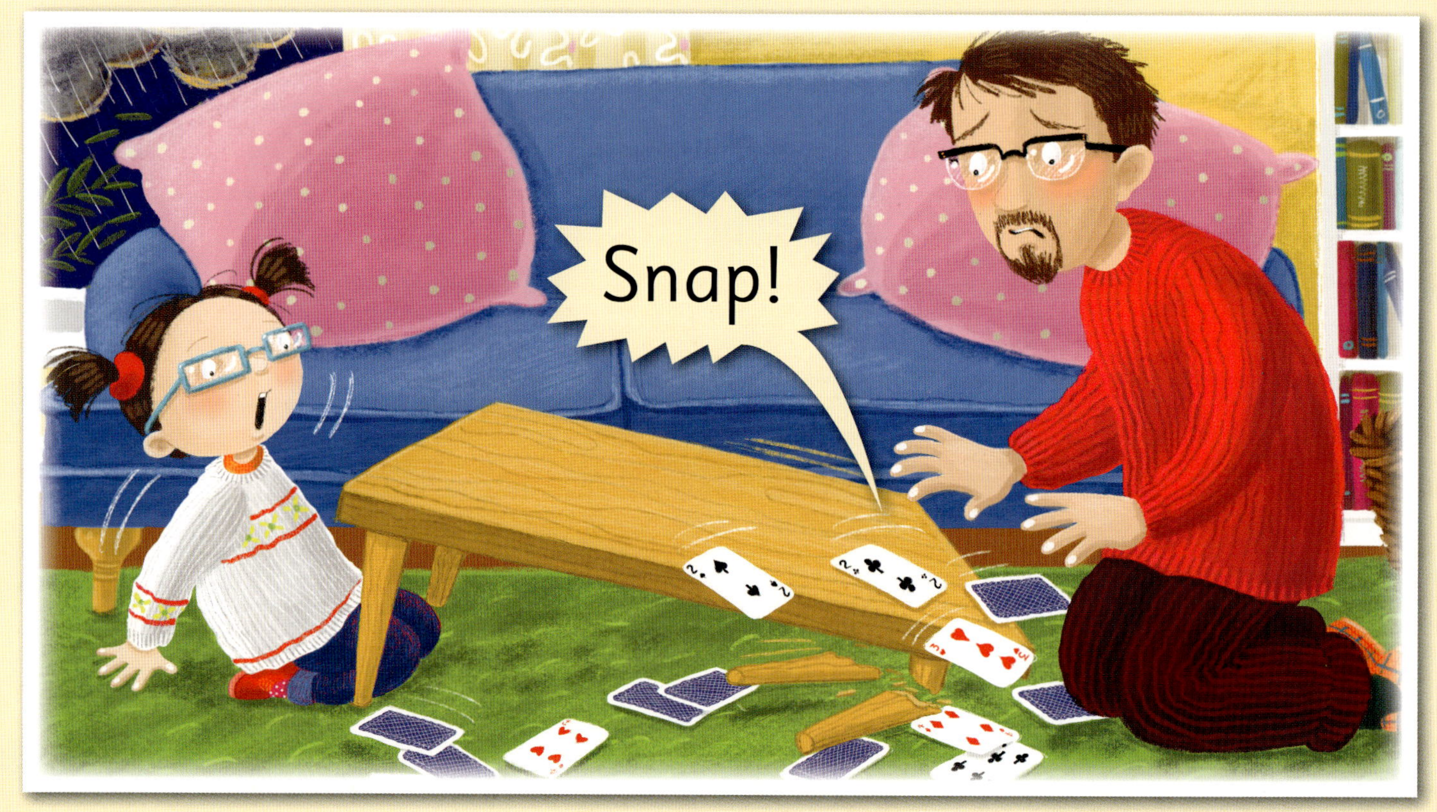


Tip!